A Sudden Swirl of Icy Wind

Also by Anne Fine

for older readers

*Available in Mammoth

Anne Fine

A Sudden Swirl of Icy Wind

Illustrated by David Higham

mammoth

For Mary and William

First published in Great Britain 1990
by Piccadilly Press Ltd
Published 1991 by Mammoth
Reissued 2000 by Mammoth
an imprint of Egmont Children's Books Limited,
a division of Egmont Holding Limited
239 Kensington High Street, London W8 6SA

Text copyright (c) Anne Fine, 1990
Illustrations copyright (c) David Higham, 1990
Cover illustration copyright (c) Lee Gibbons, 2000

The moral rights of the author, illustrator and cover illustrator
have been asserted.

ISBN 0 7497 0255 9

10 9 8 7 6 5 4 3 2 1

A CIP catalogue record for this title
is available from the British Library

Printed in Great Britain
by Cox & Wyman Ltd, Reading, Berkshire

CHAPTER ONE

William was in the worst trouble. He was shaking as Granny towered over him, her arms folded and her face dark with rage.

"William!"

He was upset, and close to tears. But he wasn't sorry, not a bit. He had done nothing wrong. In fact, he'd been specially good, keeping himself busy in Granny's smart front room, where all the chairs were fat and stuffed and shiny, and everywhere you looked there were spindly little tables with tops as brown and gleaming as conkers, and fancy ornaments wobbling on top of them.

He hadn't knocked anything over. Nothing was broken. Nothing was even cracked. And she knew he was in here, playing with the gun he'd been given for Christmas yesterday. Mum knew he was in here, too. She had crept up on him before she left for work. She'd done one of her special vampire goodbyes, swooping to wrap him in her huge dark and flapping nurse's cloak, sinking her fangs in his soft throat.

He'd wriggled free as usual, and given her a proper kiss.

"See you tonight," she'd told him. "It's a pity that hospitals can't stop for Christmas."

Then she was off, doing her Dracula imitation on the way to the car, startling all Granny's neighbours. He'd waved from the window, then, when the car was out of sight, he'd started to prise the lid off the box that held his new gun. Granny poked her head round the door and saw him. She wasn't angry then. All she'd said was, "Happy, William?"

He'd nodded. Yes, he was happy. He'd got what he wanted most for Christmas, and he had all morning free. He knew there was more than half the cake left, and he'd be given an enormous slice as soon as Granny decided it was time for coffee. And there were game shows he liked on television later. Granny's television was much better than the one at home. So he was lucky to be here.

That's what he thought. The silver hands on the clock slid round silently as William played. Half past nine. Ten o'clock. Quarter past ten. William was getting hungrier. And then, at last, he heard Granny's footsteps tap along the hall and down the steps that led to the front room. And she was standing in the open doorway.

He turned to smile at her, and show her what he'd been doing all morning, out from under her feet, being no trouble. Proudly he said:

"Look! See what I can do. See how –"

But then he heard Granny's little gasp of shock, and saw the look on her face. First she went red, then her face darkened with rage.

"William!"

He stared.

"Just *what* do you think you are doing?"

Baffled, he looked down at the gun in his hand. But she didn't wait for an answer.

"How dare you, William!"

He couldn't think what was wrong. She knew he had the gun. She'd watched him unwrapping it beside the Christmas tree. She'd even admired the flashes of silver lightning on the handle.

"But –"

"I can't believe my eyes! So naughty! Dreadful! Shocking!"

"But, Granny –"

4

"No, William! I don't want to hear any silly excuses. I just want you to say that you're sorry."

"But –"

"Say you're sorry, William."

She stood with folded arms, waiting. William was mystified. He couldn't for the life of him work out what he'd done wrong. He hadn't made a mess or a noise. He'd been no trouble at all, just practising firing his gun over and over again, getting better and better. What was so wrong about *that*?

"William! I'm waiting!"

He glowered down at his shoes. What was she so mad about? Nothing was broken. Why *should* he say he was sorry? What had he *done*?

"William! I am still waiting!"

But William was still glowering at his shoes. No reason why he should be bullied into saying something that he didn't mean. It would be just a lie. He wasn't sorry. He was just a bit rattled with Granny standing there saying "How *dare* you?" over and over again. But how dare she try to bully someone into telling a lie?

"I'm not sorry," he muttered sullenly.

"What was that, William?"

"I said I'm not sorry!"

He didn't mean to shout it out like that. It came out loud because he was hurt and angry and a little bit frightened. He'd never seen Granny like this before. Even when he was younger and smashed her lovely china bowl of roses, doing cartwheels down the hall, she'd only blamed herself for leaving it on the table. She hadn't been angry with him. Nothing like this.

He scowled at her. She wasn't being fair.

To his dismay, she reached out and caught his arm, pulling him towards the door.

"In that case, young man, you can just sit by yourself for a while, and think it over till you *are* sorry."

She steered him across the hall towards the little room filled with old junk thrown in there years and years ago, when William's grandfather died. Tugging the door open, she pushed William in. He didn't struggle. He didn't dare. He just let her propel him forward, into the clutter. The door banged behind him, and he tripped over grandfather's

6

old sea chest, scraping his knees. He picked himself up from the floor, shaking a little, and was just sitting down on the sea chest when he heard Granny's last words coming sharply through the panels of the door:

"And don't come out till you can say you're sorry!"

Well, it would be a long wait! William had heard it often enough when he refused to wear a coat, or eat green beans, or go round to play with someone he didn't like much: "You're as stubborn as your grandfather!" It was supposed to be a joke, but it would serve Granny right if he was, and she had to wait all day.

And, sitting on the sea chest, William began to wonder for the first time in his life about the grandfather he'd never known, the famous Captain Flook. He swivelled round to take a long look at the portrait hanging, a little crooked, on the storeroom wall. Captain Flook stared out of the knobbly old wooden frame, bearded and grave. The polished buttons on his uniform caught the light, along with bands of gold lace round his sleeves, and the gold oak leaves on the peak of his cap. He was a fine-looking man. But stubborn and secretive, Granny said. If he didn't want her to know about something, he would just say: "That's between me and Mustapha".

Whatever that meant.

And this was grandfather's trunk. William had never had the chance to be alone in this room before. Granny came in sometimes to

root through the clutter of broken telescopes and cracked ships' bells, musty books in strange languages and conch shells from far-away beaches. She might be searching for a tiny spyglass so she could see better at the pantomime; or she might be hunting for some bag of old coins or pebbles or foreign stamps, to keep William busy for an afternoon. But she would always leave him in the doorway.

"Don't come in any further, William. It's such a *mess*."

So he'd never even looked in the trunk. What could be in it? It was a proper chest made of stout wood, with firm brass bands to hold it fast through all sea weathers. The clasps were stiff, and hard to lift. He'd bruise his fingers trying to prise them up. But he was determined to raise the lid and have a look inside. He'd use the edge of this strange sliver of flint, here on the floor. He'd twist it between the two halves of the clasp, and –

A sudden swirl of icy wind seemed to gust out of the chest. It smelled, quite unmistakably, of sea. William had stood often enough on slippery green rocks, staring out at the far horizon and the waves. He'd smelt the tang of sea wind and licked the salt taste of it from his lips. This was the very same wind, but it was leaking somehow out of grandfather's trunk, as William struggled to open it.

Impossible! Wind didn't *keep*. After so many years, the untouched trunk should have inside it nothing but still, stale air.

William redoubled his efforts. Gritting his teeth, he pushed harder and harder. He grunted with effort and hurt his fingers, but finally the catches gave. And with a cry of triumph

William pushed one last time, heaving until the rounded lid swung over backwards with its own great weight, and hit the floor with a crash.

The smell of sea filled the whole room. The air around was suddenly chilly and windy and wet and fresh, and William could taste salt spray.

And there, inside the trunk, lying on rotting sacks, was an old bottle. An old green bottle, made of glass, but of a glass so ancient and dark and pitted that William could not begin to guess what might be hidden inside it.

Gingerly he rolled it over on the sacking. It felt chill to the touch. What was inside? As Granny said, his grandfather was far too secretive. He should have labelled it. Then William would not have had to lift it out – oh, so carefully – and hold it, colder than a stone in his hand, while he twisted at the encrusted glass stopper. What was it grandfather always said when he chose to keep a secret?

"That's between me and Mustapha."

Such a curious thing to say. So foreign and exotic. And suddenly William found himself softly saying the word aloud, testing the strangeness of it out on his own tongue.

"Mustapha."

Then, just a little louder:

"Mustapha."

Then, louder still:

"Mustapha. Mustapha! *Mustapha*!"

There was another swirl of icy wind. The smell of salt grew stronger, and William could have sworn he heard the lonely cry of a sea bird. The room seemed to heave, as if the floorboards had become a ship's deck, and the storeroom itself was suddenly afloat on the high seas.

Then, with a crack, the stopper of the bottle split in two. Each half of shattered glass began to melt into a mist, green as the bottle itself. And from the bottle poured more mist, and more and more, until it was as thick as fog, and a green pillar of it coiled and rose, up and up, higher and higher, until it was high as the ceiling.

As William stared, the thick green fog gathered itself into a shape, the strangest shape, a towering and turbaned man of mist. His chest was beefy and his shoulders broad.

13

His arms were folded across his massive body. But in the coiling vapour of his lower half, there were no legs at all, not even the shape of them. Only a spiral of thinning green mist, trailing back into the bottle.

The vision towered above William.

"I am Mustapha," he said. "The genie of the bottle. Someone has called me."

CHAPTER TWO

Transfixed with terror and astonishment, William could not speak. The genie loomed above him. After a moment's silence, he spoke again.

"You have only to command me."

But command him what? To pour the vapour of himself back in the bottle, safe out of sight, and bring the world to rights again? Well, not to rights, exactly. Nothing was right today. And, thinking this, William stood still and silent as, one by one, tears of fright and exhaustion rolled down his cheeks.

The genie unfolded his beefy arms and, leaning over, reached down to touch William's cheek with a chilly mist finger. He lifted a tear.

15

"You are in trouble."

It wasn't even a question. But still William nodded.

The genie glanced round the storeroom.

"Where are the sofas of feathers and rose petals?" he asked. "The silken hangings and the swaying fans? The sweet music and the lovely dancing girls? The jugs of wine, the dishes of fat geese drowned in sweet berry sauce? Are you *imprisoned*?"

If you looked at it that way, thought William, he practically was. And awash with misery and self-pity, he somehow couldn't help nodding a second time.

"Tell me your gaoler's name!" the genie cried. "Prayers and regrets shall be out of season! I shall heap piles of stones upon his head!"

"Actually, it's my granny," said William.

"Your own grandmother! You astonish me! Tell me to wing her to a stony place inhabited by wolves. Her body shall be carrion for the crows, prey for the beasts!"

"She didn't mean it," William said hastily. "Honestly. She was just a bit cross."

"Cross?"

16

"Well . . . Furious, really."

The genie settled himself more comfortably on his spiralling coils of mist, and listened carefully as William, gradually pushing aside his fear of the huge shape towering above him, explained how the trouble had started. How, by the time Granny poked her head round the door to invite him for cake and coffee, he had been practising with the gun for hours, firing the six little pellets over and over again, getting better and better, till, if he aimed at the tiny plastic cow, then that was the only animal that fell over. And if he aimed at the little man with the crook, the shepherd, it was he who went spinning over backwards onto the cotton wool snow. If he aimed at the angel, she tumbled off the stable roof. And if he closed one eye and kept his hand as steady as possible, he could even hit something as small as the legs of the ox and ass's feeding trough, and send the tiny plastic baby, in a shower of straw, catapulting out of the manger.

"Manger?" The genie's look of bafflement was turning slowly into one of shock. "Did you say 'Shepherd? Angel? Ox and ass? *Manger*?'"

"They're only plastic," said William. "And

17

they're not even new. And every time I'd knocked them down, I set them all up again, exactly the same. I even picked all of the straw off the carpets. I can't imagine why she made such a fuss."

He looked up to see the genie's face darkening with rage. All William's terror returned. What could a genie do if he lost his temper? Did he have to wait for a command? Perhaps, now he finally realised just how unfair William's granny had been, he might suddenly wing her away and heap her with stones.

"She's usually very nice," said William. "She's usually very patient."

"Powers of heaven!" the genie cried. He seemed to be swelling as if, as his anger grew, he had to grow to hold it. "Clearly if your grandmother's patience was as deep as the sea, you would still try to swim beneath it."

It took William a moment to make sense of this. But when he understood what Mustapha meant, he was indignant.

"Why pick on *me*? What have *I* done?"

The genie looked at him with deep disdain.

"It seems, to start, you have been born when wits were scant."

"Are you calling me stupid?"

The genie folded his arms and stared imperturbably into space.

"*Jawab ul ahmaq sakut*," he murmured. "The only answer to a fool is silence."

William was no coward. And he was suddenly sick of everyone around him folding their arms and going dark in the face for no good reason he could understand. So, folding his own arms in insolent imitation, and glaring up at the genie in his turn, he shouted at him:

"I have only to command you. That's what

19

you said. I command you to stop being rude, and answer me. What have I done wrong?"

The genie glanced down. Was he taken with William's courage, or his foolhardiness? Whichever it was, the look on his face suddenly changed, softening from haughty contempt to interest in this boy who had the boldness to stand up and bellow at a genie whose powers of enchantment had, over centuries, held kings and sultans in awe.

And then he pursed his lips, and blew. A sudden swirl of icy wind chilled the room, making poor William shiver. And, as he watched, the genie began to shrink. First William thought Mustapha had decided to disappear. Then he realised the genie was simply choosing to blow the bulk of his damp self away, and make himself smaller. Harder and harder the genie blew, and the wind swept round colder and colder. Mustapha sank – lower, lower, lower – till, man-sized, he settled comfortably on Captain Flook's trunk.

"Come. Sit beside me on your father's sea chest."

William hesitated before daring to correct him.

"It was my grandfather's. And he died a long time ago."

Mustapha sighed.

"Life is a splendid robe," he said. "Its only fault is its short length."

William perched nervously on the very edge of the chest, and tried to reply in Mustapha's own way of speaking.

"Your robe must be quite long, though."

The genie stared, unsmiling, back through centuries, and into ages yet to come.

"The robe of enchantment has neither seams nor hem."

Did he mean that a genie lives forever? That would explain how he could rise from a trunk in which he'd wasted years and years, and not seem to mind about half a lifetime missed.

William pointed to the portrait.

"So it was grandfather you knew?"

"And his father. And his father, too. Men of honoured memory." Mustapha pointed an accusing finger at William. "Not one of them would shame himself the way you have today."

William spread his hands in exasperation.

"What have I *done*?"

"A droplet of advice," the genie said. "A

man's religion is like his table. One eats off fine white linen, another off scrubbed wood. Some set a feast, and others eat only the most simple dishes. This man will eat in silence, and these ladies eat with song and dance. Would you spit in the food?"

"Spit in the food? Of course not!"

The genie fell silent and waited while William thought. Did what the genie said make any sense? Had he done something as horrid and upsetting as spitting in someone's food? William thought back. It was true that Granny cared about her battered nativity stable and the little figures. Each year she lifted them carefully from the box, and set them up on the side where everyone could see them. And after Christmas she packed them away just as carefully. They certainly weren't expensive. William had seen them often enough in the shops, and they were half the price of those fierce fighting figures everyone in his class used to collect and paint, before they took up with the guns. So they must be precious in a different way. And the longer William sat quietly beside Mustapha, thinking about it, the clearer it all was.

Granny went to church. She went at Easter and at Christmas, and sometimes on Sundays. She kept a cross beside the bed, and she'd been married in church. And once, when the film of Jesus's life came on television, she'd asked William to sit quietly or slip off somewhere else. She was a Christian. She believed in God, and she believed Jesus was God's son. So that tiny plastic baby in the manger meant something to Granny. Something very important. Mustapha was right. Flipping it head

over heels with a pellet from a gun was probably even ruder and more hurtful than spitting in food.

William felt terrible – shabby and thoughtless and ashamed. More tears forced their way out and rolled down his cheeks, and, once again, the genie stretched out a finger to catch one.

"Another droplet of advice," he said. "He that respects not cannot be respected."

"I feel simply awful," said William.

The genie smiled.

"May Allah dry your tears and raise your spirits. Wisdom walks slowly, but her steps are sure."

William was unconvinced.

"You said grandfather, and his father, and his father too, would never shame themselves the way I have today."

"No family rocks nothing but angels in the cradle," the genie said. "Perhaps Captain Flook the Adventurer lives a second time in you."

"Which one was he?"

The genie shrugged, and William realised Mustapha neither knew nor cared how many fathers' fathers came between William and Captain Flook the Adventurer. Again he seemed to stare back, through centuries of magic, to grander days in his own land.

"Tell me," said William, settling on an old rug rolled on the floor beside the sea chest. "Tell me the story."

The genie stirred.

"You have only to command me . . ."

CHAPTER THREE

"Your great, great, great, great, great –" He hesitated a moment, and then shrugged. "One of your grandfathers –"

"Of honoured memory!"

"Was a fine sailor called Captain Flook the Adventurer. And he commanded a fine ship and followed the four winds on seas blackened by storm and frosted by moonlight. He took his ship further than any other, past where the whales whistle and the porpoises roll, and he was always the first to see strange things."

William hugged his knees.

"I know," he said. "Granny has an embroidery hanging above her bed. I learned it when I had chicken pox. It says: *They that go down to the sea in ships, and do business in great waters, these see the works of the Lord and his wonders in the deep.*"

"Exactly so," agreed Mustapha. "And Captain Flook saw many wonders and sailed many seas. But no man holds the wind in his hands, and there came a day when not a breath stirred in his ship's sails. And another day. And another. And for weeks afterwards the ship rocked only at the mercy of the waves, while the tar bubbled in her seams from the heat, and the decks cracked, and the crew turned from men to living skeletons. Then, out of spite, a wind rose into a cruel squall which tore the sails into a thousand pieces, and drove the ship on rocks, and all the men that were not starved were drowned."

"But not him."

"Not him. A wave lifted her white neck, and dropped the Captain on the sands of an island. And it was there, searching for water, that Captain Flook found an old bottle –"

"And pulled out the stopper!"

"And freed your servant from a thousand years of idleness."

William closed his eyes as Mustapha told his story, and saw the mist that poured out of the bottle, causing Captain Flook to stumble back on the shingle in his astonishment. He saw the fog that rose, up, up and up, making the sea boil, till it reached high as the clouds and towered darkly over the ocean and the land, before it took its ancient, magic shape.

"Was he as scared as I was?"

"He did me the honour of appearing so."

"And when he stopped being frightened, what did he want?"

Mustapha snorted.

"Trifles and toys: jugs of crystal water, a loaf of bread; and afterwards rubies, sapphires, riches of all kinds – oh, and of course, a magic carpet."

"To fly to a safe place!"

"No place boasts safety." The genie shook his head. "I bring a man only the lesser gifts of treasure and luxury. The two great gifts are not within my power."

"The two great gifts. What are they?"

"Wisdom and Life."

William thought about it for a moment. It made sense. Then he looked up, and saw Mustapha watching him with a little smile.

"Go on," William ordered. "Carry on with the story."

The genie bowed his head.

"You have only to command me. The carpet flew over India and over Persia. It flew over Syria and Egypt, and all of Arabia. It flew over a dozen great deserts and a dozen great cities. And all the while Captain Flook the Adventurer was hungry for more treasures: bags of gold, strings of pearls, dishes of diamonds. And he piled them round him on the magic carpet till he was satisfied at last. And then he leaned over and pointed to a courtyard far below, with fountains and shady palm trees."

"And that's where you brought the carpet down to land."

"Indeed, he had only to command me. The carpet circled the high minaret tower on which the muezzin stood, calling the faithful to prayer. And it came gently to rest on firm ground, under the branches of a spreading tamarind tree."

"Were the people astonished to see him?"

"Nobody saw."

"Was no one there?"

"The courtyard was filled with people. It was noon on the last day of the week, and everyone had come to pray. There were so many worshippers that those who could not fit inside the mosque had unfolded their prayer mats on the stones of the courtyard."

"To make their own little holy place!"

31

"To make their own little holy place. And, turning towards Mecca, their holiest place of all, they said their prayers to Allah the Beneficent, the Merciful, bowing their heads to the ground."

"And so they didn't notice Captain Flook."

"No. They were deep in prayer. And he, dizzy from flying through air, didn't see them. He stood and stretched and yawned, and felt the good hard ground beneath his feet. And his thoughts turned at once to his treasures, and what they might be worth. So hastily gathering up all the gems he could, Captain Flook stepped out of the shade into sunlight."

"Didn't they notice him then?"

"No. But now, at last, the Captain noticed them. For at that very moment the Minister of the Mosque, the Imam, began to read aloud from the holy book. *'The east and the west is God's,'* he declared. *'Therefore, whichever way you turn, there is the face of God. Truly, God is immense and knowing.'*"

"It sounds like something Granny might embroider," said William.

Mustapha shrugged. "A Christian reads the Bible, a Moslem the Koran, a Jew the Torah. Lose one book, and you could reach God with another. The stones that build all the great faiths are much the same. Only the rooftiles and the decorations differ. I have seen good men everywhere, and everywhere a good man is known for what he is."

"So they wouldn't mind the Captain being in their courtyard?"

"Not in the slightest. The Captain would have been welcome. But when he heard the Imam's voice, he spun around in surprise. The dish of gems flashed in the fierce sunlight, and the Captain was dazzled. Stumbling, he showered over the bent backs of the worshippers a cascade of diamonds and emeralds, sapphires and amethysts, rubies and opals, crystals and pearls."

William's eyes widened.

"Did he go after them?"

"Indeed he did." Mustapha's lip curled. "Scrabbling and snatching, tripping and cursing."

"Cursing?"

"Yes, cursing. Even as the faithful were at prayer."

It made shooting little pellets at a plastic crib look like pretty mild stuff. William felt rather cheered as Mustapha went on with the story of how Captain Flook the Adventurer fell in such deep trouble.

"At first, no one moved, such was their shock and disgust. Then, as even the Captain realised his foolishness, and left off his hunt for gems, there was the most terrible silence. The only sound to be heard was the faint clatter of a diamond here, the soft roll of a pearl there. And then, as the Imam took up his reading of the Koran again, Little Cassim Ali who sold burnt peas in the market place leaped to his feet. He signalled to his friend Zantout, who watered the streets to lay the dust. And together they turned their eyes on Abou Mekares who was the strongest man in the Caliph's guard. And without a word the three of them seized Captain Flook, who had only a moment to kick the old green bottle safely away under the tamarind tree."

"Where did they take him?"

"To the prison nearby, where he was locked up so that he could no longer disturb their holy prayers."

"Just like me, really," said William. "And for upsetting people in exactly the same way."

"As I dared to suggest," Mustapha reminded him. "Perhaps the Captain lives a second time in you."

"We've got it a bit better this time, then," said William. "Being stuck in here can't be half as bad as being in prison."

Mustapha raised an eyebrow.

"Forgive me," he murmured. "But truth is not hid in a nutmeg. Compared with this place, the prison was a palace brimming with pleasure and luxury."

Maybe the storeroom wasn't the best room in Granny's house. Or the tidiest. But even so, William felt duty bound to defend it.

"That isn't very polite. How could a prison be better than here?"

In answer, Mustapha just murmured:

"*Kas na guyad ki dugh-i-man tursh ast . . .*"

"What does that mean?"

"Nobody calls his own buttermilk sour . . ."

William was irritated.

"Tell me," he ordered, "how Captain Flook could be better off in his prison than I am here."

Mustapha bowed his head. "You have only to command me. First, in his prison Captain Flook found a dish of weevils feasting on rotten barley bread. Here, there is nothing – indeed, a man's belly might begin to fear his throat was cut."

William was still unravelling this when Mustapha continued:

"Second, in prison the Captain had the company of forty learned men. Here, before I arose –"

"Forty learned men? In a *prison*?"

"Most certainly. And most learned. All doctors."

"All doctors! How?"

"Perfectly simple. The Caliph was weak and sickly. So with the rising of each moon, he summoned a doctor and demanded a cure. Then, as the moon waned and he felt no better, he threw the doctor in prison."

"Forty doctors, though! That's longer than three years of being ill. What on earth was wrong with him?"

Mustapha sniffed.

"Everything and nothing. Nothing and everything. Everything because the man was weak almost to death. Nothing because the cause was a lifetime of idleness. The Caliph had young girls to fan him and young boys to lift the spoon up to his lips. He had women to bring him his robes and dress him, and men to carry him from place to place. From the moment his honoured mother gave him birth, the feet of the Caliph had never touched the ground."

"Never touched the ground!" William was shocked. "I don't believe it!"

"I can assure you that it was the truth. The soles of his slippers were made of the finest silver tissue."

William rocked on the carpet, hugging his knees and gazing at his own tough winter shoes. Slippers of silver tissue! Ridiculous! Glancing up at Mustapha, he asked:

"Didn't any of the doctors *notice*? Didn't they *guess*?"

"Guess? They were all fine doctors. They all *knew*. But none of them dared say."

It made sense. William would not have wanted to be the first to tell a mighty Caliph that he was actually a lazy slug.

"Tricky . . ."

A hint of admiration crept into Mustapha's voice.

"It was a puzzle to test even a genie's powers. And I, alas, was trapped in my bottle under the tamarind tree. But Captain Flook was a resourceful man, and he who must face the terrors of tides and rocks and angry seas must learn courage and quick wits. So when the Captain heard the doctors' story, he stood and rattled the bars of the prison, and shouted for the guard.

'Take me to the Caliph!' he roared.

'Why?' laughed the guard. 'Is your body in such a hurry to say farewell to your head?'

'Take me to the Caliph!' roared the Captain again. 'Or it will be your head rolling over stones, not mine. I have sailed across a dozen seas to bring the Caliph a cure for his weakness.'

'A cure for the Caliph's weakness?' The whisper ran around the prison walls. 'He brings a cure across a dozen seas.'"

William looked up.

"I bet the guard took him to the Caliph pretty sharpish once he heard that."

Mustapha agreed.

"So fast the Captain barely saw the chambers of polished black marble through which he was hurried. And, finally, he stood before the Caliph."

"What did the Caliph say?"

"Hardly a word. The Caliph lay on a sofa of the finest brocade. Too weak to raise head or finger, he simply whispered:

'Give me the cure.'

'Alas,' said the Captain. 'I cannot give it to you. For the cure is the key of good health, and it lies buried in your palace garden.'

'Send for it quickly,' whispered the Caliph. 'For I am weak almost to death.'

'Alas,' said the Captain. 'The key to good health cannot be found by another. The one who digs for it, and finds it, takes the cure.'

"The Caliph lay back, exhausted and disappointed, as his last hopes drained from his

41

face. But the Captain had quite as much to lose as the Caliph in this matter, so he stepped forward.

'Come,' he said in the voice that had soothed many a ship's boy through his first tempest. 'Let us go in the garden and look for the key.'"

"And did he go?"

"Trembling, the Caliph took the weight of his body on his own feet for the first time in his life. As he stepped forward, resting on the Captain's arm, the slippers of silver tissue fell away in shreds. Barefoot, he shuffled weakly down the marble steps, into the garden. And there the Captain took a spade from the hand of an astonished gardener, and handed it to the Caliph.

'Dig.'

'Where?' asked the Caliph, spilling hot tears in his weakness. 'The garden is huge. Where shall I find this key of good health?'

'Alas, nobody knows.'

'But,' cried the horrified Caliph. 'I might dig the whole garden before I find it!' He turned to the Captain, but the Captain simply bowed his head, and stood in silence. And so, slowly and sadly, the Caliph lifted the heavy spade and let

it drop in the earth. Slowly and sadly he bore his weight down on the handle, lifting a clod of dry earth. Slowly and sadly he bent over and sifted through it.

'Nothing,' he said.

'Try again,' begged the Captain in the voice that had encouraged many a ship's boy up the highest mast. And, strengthened, the Caliph dug – once, twice, three times – until the Captain said:

'Enough. Let us rest. The key of good health will not disappear. We'll dig again tomorrow.'"

William was grinning hugely.

"Brilliant!" he interrupted Mustapha. "Brilliant! And did the Caliph go out and dig the garden every day?"

Mustapha chuckled in turn. "Every day for a whole month. And every morning he asked the Captain: 'Shall we find the key of good health today?' And every morning the Captain replied: 'Perhaps, if we dig deep enough and long enough.'"

"And the Caliph got stronger and stronger!"

"The weakness dripped from him as from a melting rose sherbert. His flabby arms grew muscled and strong. His soft belly vanished. His legs grew wiry and brown. Some days he dug for hours and, in the sheer pleasure of digging, forgot the key."

"And the Captain didn't remind him?"

"Not for a moment. The Captain lolled on the steps of the fountain, sipping lush wines and trying to decide if Fatima, the jewel of the harem, would make a sailor's wife. Sometimes, watching the Caliph dig, he felt his own muscles weakening from disuse, and, leaping up, he'd try to wrestle the spade from the Caliph's hand."

"Wrestle it?"

"Indeed, yes. The Caliph had become a strong man with all his digging. Not wishing to give up the spade, he'd wrestle back. And the two men might struggle happily for hours over one spade, till one day the grand vizier tired of the sight and, without thinking, sent for another. As soon as the Caliph saw it, he cried: 'What? Another spade? But then the Captain might be the lucky man who finds the key of good health!'

'Sovereign of the Faithful,' said the grand vizier, shaking his head. 'Do you not know that you do not *need* the key any longer?' The Caliph stared at the grand vizier in amazement. Then he looked down at his strong lean arms and his firm legs, and tears of happiness sprang in his eyes, and he turned to Captain Flook the Adventurer.

'Ask me for anything,' he said. And, promptly, the Captain answered:

'Give me a ship, a wife, and that old green bottle that lies under the tamarind tree in the courtyard beside the great mosque.'"

"And so the Caliph let him go?"

"He was a man of honour. He kept his word."

"And the three of you sailed off."

"We all sailed off. The Captain sailed proudly, bathed in the heartfelt praises and grateful blessings of all the Caliph's people. Fatima sailed with her eyes tightly closed, pale as a grub, leaning over the ship's rail. And I lay, greener than mist, inside the sea chest on a bed of the finest brocade."

"That rotten sacking?"

"It is past its best."

"Why didn't the Captain let you out of the bottle? You could have helped poor Fatima."

Mustapha smiled.

"The Captain had learned his lesson. A gift given brings very little and does not last. A gift earned brings more, and lasts a lifetime.

46

Fatima opened her eyes after a week, and saw the dolphins wheeling and leaping in the high green seas."

"*His wonders in the deep . . .*"

Mustapha bowed his head.

"*Lakum dinukum wa li dini,*" he murmured. "To you your religion, and to me mine."

"What if you haven't got one?" William was thinking about himself and his mother.

Mustapha shrugged.

"What a man thinks, or does not think, is his own business. It's what a man does in the world that counts."

Mum was all right, then. She spent half her life up at the hospital, stitching up cuts and helping frightened people. He wasn't quite so sure about himself, going round upsetting people. The memory of Granny's folded arms and dark face came back to William in a horrid rush.

"I'm not doing so well, am I? Granny was so angry. Grabbing my arm and pulling me along and pushing me in here." He sighed. "But now that I know what upset her, I think I could say sorry."

Mustapha sniffed.

"And she could usefully return the favour."

"What? Granny? Say sorry to *me*?"

William was amazed.

"Why not?" Mustapha shook a finger towards the door. "Grey hairs do not come woven into a halo. And no one should go poking in another's bag, looking for sins. These things are best left to God."

Mustapha had a point. There were enough religions in the world, and they all cared about different things – here a cross, there a scroll; what you ate, how you dressed, which way you faced when you were praying, words you said. You couldn't keep everyone's rules if you tried. You would always be in trouble with *someone*.

"And Granny didn't even bother to try to explain, before she lost her temper."

Suddenly Mustapha seemed bored with the whole sorry business. He yawned a small cavern of mist. And another.

"For every believer found sitting peaceably in God's house, you will find three more fighting on the steps," he said. "As you will see when you are old enough to go to sea."

"Me? Go to sea?"

Mustapha stared. A sudden swirl of icy wind chilled the room. Was he annoyed? Certainly the look on his face had turned to stone.

"Are you a Flook? Or are you not?"

"Well, yes. I suppose I am. I'm William Flook –"

William broke off. Mustapha was swelling – up and out and off the sea chest towards the ceiling. The cry of gulls rang in William's ears. The floorboards heaved. There was a salt taste on his lips and, far away, he could hear the crash of surf.

Filling the room with his sea mist, Mustapha roared:

"Am I to lie *forever* in this trunk? How many Flooks must live and die before I see again the crescent moons and desert sands of my first days?"

"I'll take you back!" cried William. He'd promise anything. Anything to stop the sound of surf crashing on rocks, harder and harder, so any moment Granny would appear at the door. "I'll take you back, I swear. If I'm a sailor, you'll see them with me. If not, I'll go once and leave the bottle there."

"Your word on it!"

The genie stretched down to William a clammy hand of mist. His piercing eyes were green as deepest seas, and, as if hypnotized by the sheer power of his glance, William tucked his own hands safely behind his back, and lowered his head.

"You have only to command me," he said simply.

Mustapha laughed. The laughter echoed as he gathered himself up on his coils of mist. It turned to the harsh cry of a sea bird as, with another swirl of icy wind, he spun around, pouring himself back in the bottle. Faster and faster he spun. And as the mist flowed downwards, clearing the air and emptying the room, the cry of the sea bird grew fainter and fainter, more and more far away. Until, as the last wisps of green mist formed themselves into a stopper, and hardened instantly to pitted glass, the room was filled with silence.

"William?"

William turned. Granny was standing in the doorway, looking anxious.

"William, what was that noise? Are you all right?"

He looked down at the bottle, lying so harmlessly on its bed of rotten sacking. *Was* it the finest brocade, past its best? Was –? Did –? Had –?

There would be time enough. And there'd be time to keep his promise, too. Carefully, William lifted the heavy lid of the sea chest and swung it over, shutting the bottle away.

He turned to face Granny.

"I'm sorry if what I was doing upset you. I didn't realise."

"I'm sorry I was so angry. I didn't think."

She stretched out her arms. Gratefully, William walked towards her. She slid an arm round his shoulders as they strolled out of the room together. There was still time for cake and coffee and the game shows on television. His mother would be back later. The day was saved. As for the future, William had time to think about that. There was no need to talk about it now. After all, William found himself thinking as they walked down the hall, 'That's between me and Mustapha'.

Whatever that meant.

Parenting the ADD Child